Emma—
Never forget, yo[u]
can do ANYTHI[N]...

▽ Ali:

You Can Do Anything!

Written by
Steven Hattamer

Illustrations by
Stacy Heller Budnick

Published by Raggedy Man Productions
All Rights Reserved
Paperback ISBN: 978-1-7333884-0-5
Hardcover ISBN: 978-1-7333884-2-9
Ebook ISBN: 978-1-7333884-3-6

For Beth, Ali, Hannah, Miss, and Jack—thank you for being my family and reminding me that, with your love, I can do anything!

Once upon a time, there lived a nice family, just like yours. They were just like yours because they loved each other very much.

Theirs was a home full of laughter and joy and music. Together, the family would dance and play, enjoying each other's company.

Each night as Mom and Dad tucked in the kids, they would say:

"You are a GOOD person.

You are SMART . . .

You are TALENTED . . .

You are BEAUTIFUL . . .

You are STRONG . . .

*and **YOU can do anything!**"*

Every night, from the day they were born, the children would hear these words. Sometimes Dad said it. Other times Mom said it. Sometimes the children said it to each other. When they heard it after the lights went out, it always made them giggle, 'cause Daddy would whisper it in their ears, and it always tickled!

Not a night passed without those words, and they became a part of each child until they could no more forget those words than they could forget their own heads!

Sometimes, when their brother and sister were sleeping, Ali and Hannah would sneak downstairs to listen to their parents' talk.

"You are talented," Mom would tell Dad.

"You are beautiful," Dad would tell Mom.

Hearing their parents use those special words made the girls feel happy and safe.

One day in school, Ali's teacher handed out a test. Ali silently read the first question. She could already see that this was the hardest test she had ever taken.

Looking around the room, she saw worried looks on the faces of her classmates.

I don't know if I can do this, Ali thought.

Just then, Ali heard a small voice deep inside her.

You are SMART!

Ali knew that voice. And she knew it was right. *I* can *do this. I* can *do anything!* she thought.

Ali focused on the test. As she worked, she realized that it wasn't so hard, after all.

Walking home that day, she realized her parents were right: if she believed in herself, she *could* do anything!

The next week, Hannah had her first piano recital. She was about to step onstage when, suddenly, her heart began racing. Her hands grew damp, and she felt a lump the size of a goose egg in her throat. Hannah had never played in front of so many people, and lots of them were strangers. She was frozen in place.

Forcing her feet to move, she stumbled out from behind the curtain. The audience stared at her, waiting for her to begin. She swallowed, and the lump in her throat grew even bigger.

Then she saw her whole family in the front row. She remembered how much fun it was to play for them at home. She liked playing for them because they would dance and sing and just be silly!

Looking at her excited family, she thought of those words they said to each other every night. From deep inside, she heard,

You are TALENTED!

The voice started getting louder and stronger until, finally, Hannah said to herself, *I can do anything!*

Hannah beamed a beautiful smile at the audience. Then, taking a seat, she played the piano as if she were sitting at home with her family. It was fun! As the audience clapped, she realized Mom and Dad were right. If you believe in yourself, you really *can* do anything.

A few days later, Missy was playing on the playground. She missed a handle on the monkey bars and . . . PLOP!!!! Down to the ground she went.

The other kids started to laugh and make fun of her.

Missy looked down and saw her favorite shirt covered in mud. Tears welled in her eyes. She was a mess!

Then she heard a small voice from deep inside, saying,

You are BEAUTIFUL!

Missy remembered Dad telling her that beauty was more than skin deep—that real beauty came from within and was about being brave and fearless. Missy looked down at her clothes again. Who cared if she was dirty? It was just dirt!

Brushing herself off, she stood and reached for the monkey bars again. As she swung past the other kids, she felt an incredible strength in her arms and a joy in her heart at overcoming a bad situation.

Not long after, Jack was playing soccer. He and his teammates tried as hard as they could and used every ounce of their strength, but they could not beat the other team.

Jack and his friends were very disappointed. A few of his teammates were so upset that they didn't even want to shake hands with the other players.

Suddenly, Jack heard a small voice in his head, saying,

You are STRONG!

Jack realized that Dad hadn't just been talking about the kind of strength it takes to play a tough game of soccer. He'd also been talking about the strength in your heart and soul—the kind of strength it takes to smile when you're sad and shake hands when you don't want to be friendly.

As he took his opponent's hand, Jack said, "Good game!"

Jack thought, *Dad was right. I can do anything!*

One day, the kids noticed a commotion at school. Older boys were picking on Jeff, the new boy in Jack's class. The bigger boys were pushing him and teasing him about his shabby clothes.

All of a sudden, a blond blur flew by. Before the girls knew what was happening, Jack was between Jeff and the big boys. Ali, Hannah, and Missy joined Jack and Jeff, staring defiantly at the bullies.

The older boys decided it wasn't worth their trouble and ran off.

Jeff thanked the kids for their help, but told them the boys were right. He was poor, and the shabby clothes he was wearing were his very best.

"I'm nobody special, and I'm not worth anything," Jeff said. "That's what my Dad says."

Jack and his sisters looked at each other in shock. "NO! That's not true!" they cried. "YOU ARE A GOOD PERSON!"

"That's right!" Hannah cried. "A VERY good person! And you are our friend!"

Missy said, "You are smart, talented, beautiful, strong, and . . .

Then the kids thundered all together,

"YOU CAN DO ANYTHING!"

Throughout their lives, no matter how hard things got, the children remembered those words of encouragement. And they shared them with others—they gave them to friends and to their own children as if they were gifts more precious than diamonds. Because they knew the truth: Words can help. Words can heal. If you use your words to encourage others, they will give you their hearts and show you their best. Remember . . .

You are a GOOD person.

You are SMART . . .

You are TALENTED . . .

You are BEAUTIFUL . . .

You are STRONG . . .

and YOU CAN DO ANYTHING!

Dad & Mom (Steve & Beth)

Ali   Hannah   Miss   Jack

Author

Steve Hattamer started as a high school teacher, is a physician by training, and an accidental author. *You Can Do Anything!* began years ago when the children were very young. While making up stories for the kids at bedtime and telling them that they "*could do anything,*" they said, "*Daddy, write it down and put it in a story, and we'll draw the pictures!*" Their drawings (all that could be found) have been included. Steve lives on Cape Cod and is working on his second book. For him, this book will be a colossal success if it gives even one child the spark to think that they really "*can do anything!*"

Illustrator

Stacy Heller Budnick is based out of New York City. She created the art for *You Can Do Anything!* in watercolor. Stacy freelances as an illustrator while teaching full time as an art teacher in a NYC High School. Her illustration career began when she illustrated her first children's books for HayHouse publishing in 2008 and has since maintained her passion for creating images for trade and educational materials. Working on *You Can Do Anything!* has been one of her favorite projects so far!

Editor

Brooke Vitale is a children's book author and editor. She has written dozens of books, including *The Muppet Christmas Carol: The Illustrated Holiday Classic, The Magic Is in You, Disney Who's Who, Olaf's Journey,* and *Happy Birthday, Mickey.* Brooke spent more than fifteen years as an editor at prominent publishing companies, including Penguin Books for Young Readers and Disney Publishing. She now does freelance editing to allow time to raise her two young sons. Brooke can be found at BrookeVitale.com.

Designer

Katie Risor is a children's book illustrator, author, and designer based in Texas. She has illustrated and designed books such as *There's an Alligator in the Elevator!* and *When Mommy Caught a Dragon.* Katie is passionate about visual storytelling, weird creatures, and sharing art with the world. Her work can be found at www.katierisor.com

CPSIA information can be obtained
at www.ICGtesting.com
Printed in the USA
LVHW070914310121
677419LV00031B/299